Noah Henry
A Rainbow Story

Deana Sobel Lederman

TBR Books
New York

For Oren, Aiden and Liam

Today, I woke up
and got dressed for school,
but school was closed.

I packed my backpack with my teddy
and a snack for the playground, but
Mommy said we couldn't go.

I drew a picture of a fire truck
for my friend Piper, but Daddy said
I had to save it for her.

So I found my binoculars
and my hat to take to the
zoo, but the zoo was closed
too!

Mommy said we had to wash our hands.
Daddy said we had to wash our hands.
We talked to my teacher on the phone, and she
said we had to wash our hands.

I went to wash my hands.
I made my little brother Sam wash
his hands too.

Mommy gave me a hug.

"Soon, we'll be able to play with
our friends, Noah Henry" she said,
"and soon you'll be able to go
back to school. Soon, we'll be able
to go to the zoo."

Then I had an idea. "Can we take Poppy for a walk?"
This time, Mommy said yes.

We all got dressed to go outside.

The streets were mostly empty,
except…

In the window of Piper's house, we saw
a rainbow.

In the window of Reza's house,
we saw a rainbow too!

And in Aliza's window and in
Eli's window!

It was a concert of people.

It was a parade of

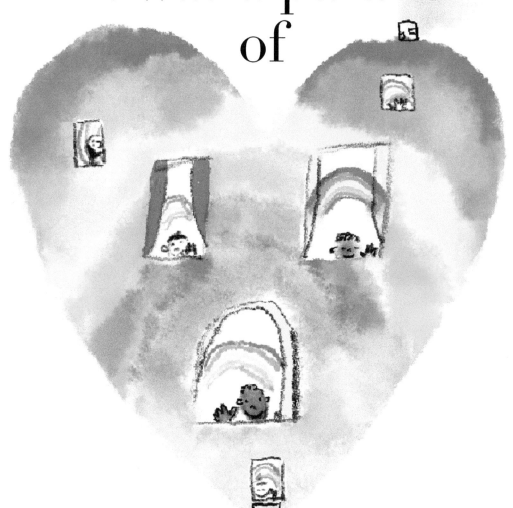

rainbows!

When we got home, I drew a
rainbow.

That night,
I fell asleep thinking of
all the rainbows and all the windows
and all the people I loved.

Deana Sobel Lederman

Deana Sobel Lederman is an author, illustrator and cartoonist. Deana's grandmother was a painter who studied at The Art Students League of New York. She taught Deana to paint with oils when she was very young, and her mother always encouraged her art. Deana drew her first cartoon, The Wacky Couples, at the age of eight and went on to become the cartoonist for UC Berkeley's student newspaper, and later a freelance illustrator and cartoonist. Later, she went to law school, where she studied copyright and patent law. Deana has lived in New York City; Mill Valley and Berkeley, California; London, England; and Cambridge, Massachusetts. She lives now in San Diego, California, where she grew up, with her brilliant husband and two little boys.

TBR Books is the publishing arm of the Center for the Advancement of Languages, Education, and Communities (CALEC), a nonprofit organization with a focus on multilingualism, cross-cultural understanding, and the dissemination of ideas. Our mission is to empower multilingual families and linguistic communities through education, knowledge, and advocacy. Visit us at www.calec.org